METTA: LET'S ME

WRITTEN BY: METTA WORLD PEACE

WITH: HEDDRICK MCBRIDE

ILLUSTRATED BY: HH-PAX

EDITED BY: MAUREEN LUNN

ISBN-13: 978-1507747841
ISBN-10: 1507747845

DEDICATION

Instilling our children with confidence and knowledge is crucial as they grow up and begin to face society on their own. At every point of contact, children are learning from the grown-ups around them—parents, relatives, mentors and public servants—all have the opportunity to set a positive example for kids and create healthy memories. It's important that our children understand the realities of racial inequality, but equally important that they understand that they are not victims of society and they hold the power to live in safety and act in confidence. That's why we wrote this story — to give kids a healthier perspective on the police force while teaching them practical, every day skills to keep them safe. This story is dedicated to police men, women, and children throughout the world who are working hard to make our society a better and safer place for all.

"Ding-dong!" the doorbell rang.

Metta was standing outside of the Boys and Girls Foster Home.

He likes to visit and hang out with the kids on the weekend. He

had something important to talk to the kids about on this day.

"Ding-dong!" Metta had to ring the bell a second time.

He didn't hear any feet running to the door like usual. Finally

Mr. Cooper, the Residence Manager, opened the door.

"Hello Metta, it's great to see you," Mr. Cooper said as

he shook Metta's hand. "The kids are in the living room glued

to the television set. They are watching the local news."

"Okay, I was wondering where everyone was," Metta

replied.

Metta walked into the living room and saw the group of

three boys and two girls watching televison.

"Hello kids, it's great to see you guys. No love for Metta today?"

"Metta!" exclaimed Timothy. "Sorry we didn't hear the doorbell. We've been watching the news all week."

"Hey Metta, how are you?" Nicole said. "It's good to see you—it's been a rough week."

"Metta, why don't the police like black people? I'm afraid of the police," Marvin expressed.

Metta shook his head and said, "No, Marvin, that's not true and there is no reason for you to be afraid. We're going to talk about this more on our trip today.

"Everyone go get ready for our trip. I promise you we'll have a good day. I have to pick up your permission slips at the front desk so I'll meet you guys outside in 10 minutes."

Metta went into the office and made sure he had all of the necessary paperwork for the outing.

Metta and the kids boarded the van. Once everyone was seated the conversation began.

"I know we have seen some troubling things on the news during the past couple of months. I want to talk to you about policemen and women today. Police are here to protect and serve our communities; they are necessary for keeping order and safety in our neighborhoods," Metta explained.

"Why do we always see them killing and hurting black people?" Marvin yelled out.

"That, or they are throwing people in jail for no reason," said Timothy.

"These are things that we have been seeing lately, but there is more to the story," said Metta. "Police officers are people just like everyone else, so there are some bad police out there, but the majority of them are good people who work hard to protect us. Police officers work in partnership with different community members to maintain law and order. They help prevent crime in our stores, homes and public places. "

"Look over there, kids. There are some police officers walking near the shopping mall to make sure those shoppers and storeowners are safe from robbers."

"Do you see that policeman over there giving that lady directions? You can tell she is lost and needs help."

As the van cruised around the neighborhood, it approached a broken stop light where an officer was conducting traffic. Metta pointed, "The policewoman is there to make sure that there are no accidents while the light is out of service."

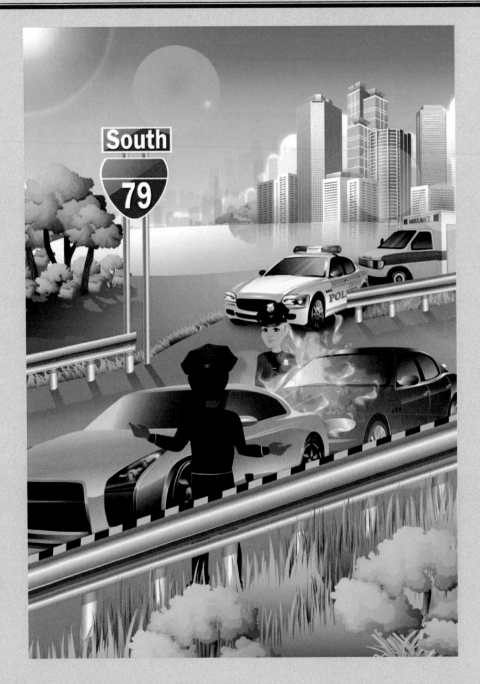

The van continued on and passed a car accident. There were two police cars and an ambulance on the scene. "The police officers are there to make sure that everyone is safe and that anyone harmed receives proper care."

The van finally pulled up in front of a big police station and the kids looked at each other. "Don't worry kids, everything will be fine," Metta assured them. The group trusts Metta so they all got out of the van.

The group walked inside of the station and was greeted by a man in uniform. "Hello, I am Captain Gonzales, nice to meet you guys. Welcome to the 25ᵗʰ precinct."

Marvin stepped forward and said, "Captain Gonzales, can I ask you a question? Do police hate black people? We hear and see it every day on the radio and television, so is it true?"

Captain Gonzales laughed and responded, "I sure hope not, because 75 percent of my partners are African American and Hispanic, and we love our family, friends and communities. We are here to protect and serve all of our citizens. I'm glad you asked that question because people usually assume things without getting all of the facts. We need to talk about things in order to know what others are feeling or thinking. Does anyone else have questions?"

Timothy spoke next. "A lot of people are saying that we should stay away from the police because they are angry and dangerous. How can we stay safe and out of trouble when we see police officers every day?"

Captain Gonzales responded, "Police officers are humans just like everyone else. We are people with feelings and emotions. We should all treat each other with kindness and respect. A policeman would be glad to shake your hand and say hello. You should give it a try."

"Our main goal is to protect and serve our communities. We are looking to stop criminals, regardless of their race. I want you kids to remember these words: education is the best protection. When you are aware of what's happening around you, you won't be afraid."

"My first piece of advice is to make sure that you all have proper identification. Even though you are under 18 years old, you should always have it. Having proper identification can protect you from being mistakenly identified in crimes, and can help you if you are lost or injured," he explained.

"The best way to avoid negative interactions with the police is to learn and follow the laws. I'm sure some kids violate laws every day simply because they're not aware and informed."

Caption Gonzales continued, "In most cities, it is illegal to ride your bicycle on the sidewalk."

"It is illegal to litter in public places. This includes throwing trash on the sidewalk or improperly dumping your garbage."

"We have some hand books here to provide you with information on some basic laws and your rights. I want you to read these and share them with your friends."

Metta said, "Before we go, let's get some identification cards made." The kids lined up one by one to get their identification cards made.

Metta walked with Captain Gonzales outside. "Thank you for talking to the kids today, Captain. They needed to hear this information."

Captain Gonzales replied, "It was a pleasure to meet your group. I am glad that we were able to give them a different view of policemen. I hope to see you at our Community Day event next month. We are having a basketball game and I would love to show you how great my jump shot is!"

Metta laughed and shook the Captain's hand. "We'll be there, only if you promise to take it easy on me."

The group waved goodbye and exited the police station. When they got back on the van, the conversation started.

"I never knew how many positive things police officers did in the community." Nicole said.

Marvin chimed in, "It's great to know that police don't hate black people—they are just trying to enforce the laws."

Greg said, "I'm glad that I got to meet the Captain. There are a lot of things that I need to learn about the law. I feel like I have more power, now that I know what could get me into trouble."

Timothy had the last word. "I never thought I would say this, but thank you, Metta, for taking us to the police station. I learned a lot today."

Everyone laughed, including Metta.

Visit www.mcbridestories.com for more titles.

Metta: Let's Meet the Police

Made in the USA
Las Vegas, NV
08 June 2022